NSFW: Not Safe For Work

By Jacqueline Applebee

http://www.writing-in-shadows.co.uk

ISBN: 978-1-4477-3449-9

Contents

Contents

The red shoes

My new shoes arrived late in the afternoon. They were bright red; patent leather with five-inch heels. They had little silver buckles on the outer edge, and when I angled the shoes this way and that, I could see my reflection in them. My new red shoes cost more than I wanted to think about. I was a part-time secretary, terribly underpaid, just like everyone else in the archaeology institute, so I should have known better, but when I'd seen them online they had practically screamed, "Buy me now!"

I was supposed to be meeting Ricky the owner of the wonderfully named, *Hot and Steamy* coffee shop; the newest addition to the caffeine-laden high street in town. It wasn't strictly a date, but if I didn't make an effort, it would never happen. For just one night I wanted to feel tall and elegant instead of short and stumpy. I was sick of being viewed as little-sister to most of the people I knew. I didn't want to bake cakes and sew dresses. I wanted to get laid. If these red shoes couldn't help me do that, I was just going to give up, wear flip-flops, and learn to love masturbation. Speaking of which, I really should have seen to my needs before I left home in the morning. I was saving myself up for something special. I bit my lip; Ricky had better be up for more than a skinny macchiato.

I removed my well-worn pumps, and then took the new shoes from their box. I winced as my toes pressed against the sides of thin leather. I had big and wide feet, so I hardly ever wore heels, and never ones that high. My feet felt constricted, but the shoes looked amazing. I imagined Ricky's broad mouth kissing the tips of the red leather, his big brown eyes gazing up at me as he licked and slurped his way up my leg. By the time his tongue reached the back of my knees, I'd be ready to hump his face into oblivion. I squirmed in my seat, sticky with anticipation.

I waved goodnight to my workmates, stole a glance at myself in the mirror on my desk, and then hurried as best as I could out of the office, though it was tricky with my new footwear. I carefully trod past my manager's office, hoping that just for once that he wouldn't give me some last-minute task that needed to done by the morning. Doctor William Gallagher was the head of the Research Institute. He could be a real slave driver sometimes, but his old-fashioned charm seemed to negate most of his bad points. It didn't hurt that he was a dashing older man with silver hair and sparkling blue eyes. He always wore a perfectly pressed suit, complete with starched white shirts and a folded hanky in his pocket. My boss's way of dress and his mannerism seemed to belong to another time. He almost seemed like one of our artefacts just waiting to be catalogued and studied. The most intriguing thing about the older man was that he'd been married three times since he'd taken over the institute ten years ago. The office gossip was that the good doctor was a ladies' man, but I couldn't see it myself. Even with his trio of ex-wives, he seemed too much of an old fuddy-duddy.

I thought I'd got away with sneaking out when the door to the doctor's office opened.

"Maria, do you think the spending report on the new acquisitions will be typed up by morning?"

I nodded, wobbling slightly.

He inclined his head. "You look different. Big night out planned?"

"Something like that," I mumbled. "Good night."

My boss shut the door behind him. "I was about to leave myself. Let me escort you outside."

I made it about three steps when my foot slipped, throwing me off balance. Doctor Gallagher held on to my elbow, steadying me for a moment.

"I'm so sorry." I felt the blood rush to my cheeks.

He shook his head. "Really, Maria, take the blasted shoes off if they're so much trouble."

"I'll be fine once I get used to them."

My boss looked down at me. I could almost hear him mentally berating me for being such a silly woman. He said nothing however, but ushered me towards the elevators. I could still see the sticky tape from the last 'Lift Broken' sign that had been taped up.

Doctor Gallagher looked at the elevator with a worried frown. "Normally I'd recommend you take the stairs, but since you're liable to break your leg, I'd advise you to not risk it."

I eyed the elevator too. The cranky old thing had broken down more times than a drama queen in search of attention. I must have stared at it for too long, because my boss prodded the button on the wall, slamming it with the palm of his hand.

"I don't think that's helping," I said nervously.

The doctor winked at me. "Don't you know it comes quicker if you treat it rough?"

I was surprised to hear such suggestive words come out of my boss's mouth. Maybe there was something to the rumours after all. He punched the button once more. The elevator doors opened magically before us. I eyed the older man as I stepped inside; he was quite fetching in the right light. Maybe my clit had taken over my higher brain functions, but the good doctor looked suddenly sexy.

The lift was tiny, with barely enough room for the two of us. My boss grinned at me as he stood close. The carriage jerked to life, moving slowly down through the floors. My feet were killing me; I would never be able to make through an entire evening in my dream shoes. "Next time I'm taking the stairs," I muttered to myself.

Doctor Gallagher nodded at my feet. "Can I ask why you're punishing yourself with such malevolent footwear?"

"I'm going out... I'm meeting someone. I wanted to wear something nice."

My boss looked impossibly shy when he next said. "I think you are lovely as you are. You don't need any special shoes to achieve that. I'm sure your friend must think the same way, or this meeting wouldn't be happening."

I turned to him, smiled at his words. "Really?"

"Absolutely. I mean, you'd be a good deal shorter without those shoes, but so what if you were? You're a fine strapping girl, Maria. Make the most of it."

"I don't think I've ever been described as strapping." I was certain that strapping couldn't be remotely sexy.

My boss loosened his tie. "You're a healthy girl, strong and vibrant. You're the sort who could take the weight of a man on top of you. Men like women with padding. Makes us feel less guilty when we act a little rough." He eyed me up and down slowly. "I've often admired your..."

"My padding?" I was sure I wasn't imagining my boss moving even closer to me.

"I admire your lovely curves." He grinned at me, but before I could appreciate his words, the lift shuddered violently, and then it went still. The lights flickered and died. We weren't moving, we weren't going anywhere.

I fumbled on the wall for the alarm button, which thankfully was still illuminated. I pressed it but nothing happened. I brought out my mobile phone, and then I dialled the number for reception on the ground floor, but there was no signal at all.

"Oh, god," I whispered. "Not this. Anything but this."

My boss reached out to pat my hand. "I'm sure the lights will come on in a moment, and we'll be on our way." He sounded unreasonably calm.

But the lights remained off, and we stayed where we were, stuck in the dark.

"I think I'll just sit down for a moment." I slumped against the side of the elevator, and then sat in a scrunched heap on the floor.

"Will you be all right, Maria?"

I reached up, held on to his hand. "I'm not usually claustrophobic." The doctor moved to squat next to me. He stroked along my calves, up to my knee. I shivered from the gentle touch. His hand swept down to my ankles. "Let's get you out of these bothersome shoes." William tugged at the offending footwear. I hesitated for a moment, but then I lifted my foot, and let him slip the evil heels from me. A wave of relief made me sigh. Why had I ever put the silly things on? And then I remembered how the magic red shoes were supposed to make me feel like a sex-bomb. Ricky was supposed to be awed by my prowess, scooping me into his arms, and then into his bed, end of story. But instead I was stuck in a metal box, trying not to freak out.

I was distracted from my thoughts when I felt William's hand on my feet. He stroked along my toes.

"What are you doing?"

"You need to relax—keep distracted from our predicament. Massaging your feet is a lovely diversion, as long as you don't mind."

I didn't mind at all. Every touch against my feet travelled straight up to my groin. William did something with his knuckles on my instep. I moaned out loud before I could stop myself.

"My third ex-wife used to love me doing this to her before..."

I inhaled a sharp breath. "Before what?"

"Before things got really interesting." William's hand slid up my skirt in a lightning-fast move. He pinched my thigh. I squeaked audibly. "I'd paddle her lovely bottom, and then I'd bend her over the kitchen counter. Adele was always a domesticated sort."

"Doctor," I gasped as two of his fingers pulled aside the lace of my knickers.

"Is this a shock to you?" he asked quite conversationally. "Why do you think I'm always giving you extra duties, trying to keep you late?" When I said nothing, he continued. "So I can watch you at work." His fingers slipped inside my cunt. I felt as if I really should say something, but I had no breath left in my throat. "You really are diligent, with plenty of stamina too. If you ever want to be my P.A, I could make it very worth your while." He yanked my knickers down with a sharp tug. I spread my legs wider, aware of my intimate scent in the confines of the broken elevator.

"That's a yes then?" I could hear the laughter in his voice.

I nodded in the dark. "What about the pay?" It was a shameless thing to ask, but I was currently in a pretty shameful situation. Asking about finances wouldn't make things worse.

"You'll get a scandalous amount of money." William slipped a thumb against my clit. "That is if you can keep up with me."

The lift trembled. At least I think it was the lift that made my body shake and convulse. I thrust forward, anchored myself fully on my boss's hand. The dark was a comfort to me; I don't think I could have gone through with it if the lights had been on. I could feel myself getting wetter, but not so wet that I didn't feel the delicious textures of his fingers as they moved and twisted inside me. I ended up kneeling over the Doctor, straddling the older man.

"My second ex-wife used to love riding my face." He pulled his fingers out of my cunt leaving me empty, but before I could urge him back inside, he bunched up my skirt. "I think it would be a thoroughly distracting thing to do."

All my good sense left me at that point. The only thing that remained was my horny, hungry body. I rose up, and then I let the doctor pull me down to him. I could feel the angle of his nose and the tickle of his moustache against my crotch. I bit my lip as his tongue made a bold sweep over my labia. The doctor's hands were strong as he steadied me by the hips. He burrowed deeper, licking and sucking. When he nipped at my flesh with sharp teeth, I grunted as if I had truly lost my mind. The lift could have plummeted to the ground with a fiery explosion at that point, but I would not have cared. The only thing that mattered was the feel of my fat clitoris as the doctor's tongue swirled round and around. I braced my hands on the metal walls, using the leverage to thrust fully against his face. He was relentless as he devoured me.

"Don't stop, please don't stop." It had been so long since I'd felt remotely like this. I just wanted it to go on forever.

My orgasm struck me like a blow. I toppled back, breathless, my heart pounding. I knew what I must have looked like, spread-eagled in the dark but I felt absolutely amazing. I didn't need any fancy footwear to feel like a sex bomb.

William held my hand, helped me to right myself. "I'm going to have to watch myself when you take up your new appointment."

"You were serious?"

"I'm a man of my word. Consider yourself promoted."

I gulped as the situation hit me. Had I just slept my way into a new job?

The lift started to shake once more, but for some reason I wasn't as terrified as I had been earlier.

A voice called out from overhead. "Is anyone in there?"

William squeezed my hand. "We've been trapped in this lift for ages!"

"Sorry, Doctor. I've been trying to get the fire rescue guys to help out, but we're not a priority. Looks like you'll be stuck for a while yet."

William sighed dramatically. "All right then. I suppose I'll have to find some way of distracting myself." He drew me close. "What will your friend think when you don't turn up to your meeting?"

I grinned to myself. "It will be okay. Ricky sees me as his little sister anyway."

William's voice was suddenly very near when he whispered, "You can be a little girl if you want, as long as I get to be the naughty boy next door." His hand cupped my breast. "My first ex-wife was a real fan of role-play."

I chuckled at the sex-crazy doctor. "Well you did say you admired my stamina."

"And your curves." He pinched my nipple. "You're a strapping girl, Maria. I insist you make the most of it."

I kissed William, smiling as I thought of all the naughty things I could do with him. And maybe I'd call Ricky and apologise the next morning, but for this night I was going to have fun. It was a direct order from my boss after all.

Shepherd Wolf

I lived in a village of fifty-five souls deep in the Scottish Highlands. There used to be more of us, but English soldiers took the able men. None of them ever came home. All who remained worked together as best as they could, but when the heat of the summer came, a fever took yet more. I was left to tend to the sick though I was no healer. My only escape was daydreams. I imagined running wild through the fields, a woman full of fury, slashing out with my fists and teeth, making the soldiers pay for what they had done. No bayonet stab could wound me. No cannonball blast could stop me. It was a wickedness and a sin to imagine such bloody carnage, but the thoughts would not go away. I knew what the daydreams meant. I knew the fate that awaited me; what would happen if a soldier ever got me alone. I wanted nothing to do with them. I preferred women anyway. I was always happier in their company.

Molly was my friend. I loved being with her, though she was always telling me what to do. "I've known you all my life, Esther," she would say to me. "And you have never had the sense to follow your instincts." Sometimes I wondered what she meant, for when she spoke she would lean over me, her breasts almost exposed in her bodice. She would stand close, so near that I could smell the hay from the fields, the butter she would churn in her mother's yard. I loved my friend dearly, but there were other feelings I was too scared to act upon. I suppose I was afraid of myself and what I was capable of. There were some instincts that I wanted to keep restrained.

The night rolled upon me, heavy as any blanket. I lay plastered to the cotton sheets in bed wet with sweat, but I couldn't sleep. I snuck down to the kitchen, a little ghost in my white nightdress. Ma had been given a ham and a jug of mead in trade for fixing an old neighbour's roof. I ate a big hunk of the meat, and then I took the jug of sweet-smelling brew. I knew full well that stealing was a crime, and I wasn't yet old enough to escape my Ma's belt if she was so inclined, but I couldn't help myself.

Once I was back in my room I took a gulp of the mead. The drink was sweet, with heat that burned my tongue and my mouth. My lips tingled. I felt hot inside and out. I heard a tap at my window, and then Molly climbed inside. She crept into bed with me, her curly hair bounced over her round face. Molly was promised to be wed to a man with a bad leg; one of the few the soldiers hadn't snatched away. My friend had a fine fat body made for birthing babies, or so my Ma had told me. I was skinny as a reed—a sore disappointment to everyone. I was eighteen, and I hadn't even started my monthly bleed. There wasn't a single thing that was right with me. I didn't want babies. And when I gazed at Molly, I didn't think of her suckling no child. I imagined myself in the crook of her arm, my face squashed to her big titties. I knew it was a wickedness and a sin, but I dreamed about it all the same.

Molly snatched the jug from me. She took a gulp and screwed up her face. "This is awful. I prefer red wine—it has more character than this slop."

"You never drank red wine. Where would you find it in a place like this?" I asked, sure that she was trying to mock me.

"My intended gave me some last week, back of the stables. He said he stole it from the English, from right under their noses."

"Liar!"

"I am not." Molly pushed me, almost made me fall out of bed. "He gave me the wine, and then he kissed me all over my neck." Molly never called her intended by his given name. I knew deep down that she didn't want a man any more than I did.

"Why would he want to do a thing like that?" I asked. I was sweating more than before, and I knew it was my friend who had affected me so.

"That's what you do when you're in love."

I tried to imagine Molly kissing her husband-to-be, but nothing came to mind. "Show me?" I moved over on the bed.

"Give me some more of that mead first." She took a long swig. I watched sweat glisten in the growing dark, dribbling down to where the buttons of her nightdress strained across her chest. And then before I knew what was happening, she climbed on top of me. My friend pushed her face to mine, pressing her lips to just below my ear. I felt her curly hair move against my throat, felt a burst of new heat from where she had kissed me. It was so good, I could scarcely breathe.

Molly whispered into my ear. "If anyone finds out, there's nothing that can save us."

"Maybe I don't want to be saved." I pulled her back, and kissed her right on the lips. She tasted hot as the ginger ale, spicy and sweet.

"Will we go to hell for this?" she asked when she drew back.

I shook my head. "I'm already in heaven." I squeezed my arms around her waist, and then I boldly moved one hand to her tits that I'd been dreaming of for more time than was seemly. Molly made a strange noise. I shushed her. "If you keep carrying on, we really will get caught."

"I cannot help it," she whimpered.

I took a handkerchief, and screwed it up into a little ball. "Bite on this." I'd seen the healer do the same thing when she stitched up my Ma last harvest. It didn't stop her from screaming, but it meant that not everyone for miles around had to listen to it.

"I need to see you." My voice was shaky. Molly cocked her head to one side, and then the meaning of my words came through. She nodded. I lifted the hem of her nightdress; the fine embroidery all girls made to their clothes went by the way. I was more interested in what lay hidden beneath. Only her intended was supposed to see this, and I knew I shouldn't take this special time from him, but I was desperate. I looked at the long white garment in my hand, and then I dared to turn my head to see my friend naked before me. Molly was beautiful. She had a wide full belly with creamy skin decorated with pale lines that squiggled this way and that. She was delicate and luscious; a very juicy woman. I bent to her, and kissed her all over her stomach, mashing her soft rolls of fat and fullness in my hands. I nuzzled her tits, and as I did, I felt a throb start between my legs. It was like thunder was trapped down there just waiting to come out. I felt a storm approaching. I pulled my friend on top of me, though I couldn't move an inch when I did. Now it was my turn to make noises like a woman possessed. Molly knelt over me, and I was able to gaze up at her sweet tits like I was staring at the moon in the ink-black sky. I wanted to howl with pleasure

"You like my bosom, don't you?" she asked, though I was sure she knew exactly how I felt.

"Aye."

Molly ground against me hard. The power in her hips

was fierce. "I like the way you say that." She bent lower. My

lips brushed against one of her juicy nipples. "My intended likes

it too. But you probably don't believe that either."

I nipped at her, caught a mouthful of her titties. "I

believe you."

"Good lass." She grabbed hold of my hands, holding

them in just one of hers. She pulled them over my head. There

was no need for it. I wasn't going anywhere. Not when I could

smell her perfume; sweat and apples ripe from the storehouse. I

wanted to say so much. I wanted to tell her that I could live out

all my days and nights right here, squashed into the mattress, hot

from the weather, and sticky from the girl. Everything I thought

I knew turned sideways as Molly's free hand moved to hitch up

the hem of my own nightdress. She looked at me just as I'd

looked at her. I prayed an earnest prayer that though I was

nothing but a skinny girl, she would see that I could love her just

as well as any man. I managed to squeeze my hands from hers, and then I yanked off my clothes in a flash. I let her press me back to the bed once more. Neither of us knew what we were doing, but we rubbed against each other, kneading and pressing until we both gasped out loud. I felt thunder move within me, but the intensity made me suddenly afraid. I froze in her arms, scared to move or even breathe.

"What's wrong?"

"Nothing." My voice sounded strange.

"Why did you stop?"

"Leave me be!" I roared. My voice didn't sound like it belonged to me; even I was shocked by the sound. Molly pulled her clothes back on in a hurry. She climbed out of the window and was gone.

****

The heat stayed with me. The next day was even worse. I felt woozy; everything seemed blurred. I didn't trust myself to be around too many people. I spent the afternoon and evening tending to one of my neighbours who was sick with the fever. She gripped my hand, stared at me with milky grey eyes. She had lost everything; the English had stolen all her sons. She had nothing left but the breath that rattled in her throat.

"You are special, Esther," she said. "Even if you are a deviant."

"I'm no deviant."

"Don't you think I can smell it on you?" She shook her head. "I'm too old to care about such things. But you, Esther, you must follow your instincts. Embrace your true nature, for it will give you life beyond your years." I didn't understand what the crazy fool was talking about; I didn't appreciate being called a deviant, but I stayed with her until she fell asleep.

I heard laughter from the door. A soldier stood there, watching me.

"Stupid women. The only time you're useful is when you're on your backs." He turned to the door, still chuckling to himself. "There's nothing here, Sergeant!" he called to another man on a horse outside. "Maybe the next village will have more than women and children."

"Well, they are not without their uses," the other man bellowed. I saw some pretty ones here. Let's stay the night, take advantage of the hospitality."

The first soldier approached me. "You look ripe enough," he said, unbuckling his belt. "A little skinny, but you'll do." He grabbed hold of my wrist, and threw me down to the floor. I felt the roll of thunder inside me once more. I rose up in the middle of the room, roared until the very walls shook. The soldier's eyes were wide with fright. He backed away but I followed him outside. My body felt on fire. I looked up to the dark sky, saw the big white moon as it hung above me. And it was then that I felt something truly change. A pain in my belly made me double over. Cramps tore through my groin. A trickle of blood snaked down my legs, painting my skin red. The horses began to snort and whine. They reared up on their legs. I felt the pulse of their hearts beating, could smell their sweat. I took a step forward; my feet carried me further than they should. One of the soldiers raised his musket, but I knocked it aside before I leapt on him. I was ravenous, and he tasted so good. Every bite I made into his lean flesh made me want only more. I heard screaming, first from the soldiers, and then from the other women in the village. I span around to see them run this way and that. They hid from me though I could smell them all, knew where each and every one of them cowered with fear. I looked to the moon once more, howled with delight, and then I ran to the trees, deep under cover.

In time I felt myself calm. The others came out of their hiding places, whispered nervously to each other about the creature that had risen from amongst them. Molly approached the trees. I stepped out to her, still covered in blood. The other women hesitantly approached me. "Wolf," they all said. "Shepherd wolf."

They led me back to the village square, washed the red stains away. They let me sleep. It was cool for the first time in months.

Molly was dozing beside me when I awoke.

"Aren't you scared of me?" I asked. She only hit me, snuggled against my front.

Another kind of hunger surfaced. I felt a growing ache between my legs. Molly's scent grew sweeter as I moved closer. After all that I had done, I felt hesitant to approach her. I didn't want to hurt her. But as I gripped her hand, and drew her to me, I could feel desire spark and flare within.

Molly blushed. I could smell the blood that collected beneath the surface of her skin. The wolf inside me wanted her, but I willed my beast to be still. Molly moved closer, turned her head so she could kiss me on the lips.

"I am not afraid of you. I trust you, Esther."

"What am I?" I whispered, looking down at my hands; the hands that had ripped flesh from bone.

"You are amazing," Molly said with a smile.

I kissed her. My tongue seemed longer than before, so I was able to lick all over her teeth and her lips. I nuzzled closer, sniffing her as I moved. My friend smelled like heaven. I lapped at her throat, bent lower to nip at her breasts. She arched and ground against me. Molly's fingers laced through my hair; the tugging sensation made my groin throb hard. I swept her petticoat up, and marvelled at the sight of her. I nosed the soft curls that lay over her skin, stretched out my tongue to taste her. It was unlike anything I had ever known, salty and sweet all at the same time. I lapped at her some more; Molly urged me on. It was strange, but I could hear the other women working outside; some of them sang, some whistled and some of them spoke in hushed tones. The little gasps Molly made were louder than anything else. I gobbled up the slick juices that gathered between my friend's legs, could feel her pulse grow quick as she gripped me and then sagged back on the bed. I spied a drop of blood on her thighs; the result of my unguarded passion. I licked the scarlet bead away with a kiss. My friend was tasty inside and out. Molly watched me as I smacked my lips.

"Did I hurt you?" I asked, though I prayed she would forgive me if I had.

"It's nothing—just a scratch, love."

I bowed my head with shame, but Molly caught me, stroked my face until I purred. "Wolf," she whispered. "My shepherd wolf. If you hurt me, then it was worth it."

****

Ma started to avoid me. It was the only true pain I felt since the change. I was wounded when her words dried up; when she could not bear to look at me. Molly's intended said he no longer wanted her either. But we had each other. We were just fine.

I still didn't understand what had happened to me, but all I knew was that I loved what I had become. I was no longer a scared lass, afraid of my own shadow. I was a fierce woman who transformed into a vengeful creature every time the full moon rose high and proud in the sky.

After a while I started to notice that Molly was changing to become more like me; she was still juicy and fat, but her strength grew with every passing day. When the English soldiers came by at the end of harvest, there were two of us to fight them off. A few other women in the village appeared at the door to my home after that, begging to be given the gift of Shepherd Wolf. Molly and I turned six of them before the winter chill came. We devoured the soldiers who hunted us, fighting until crimson splashes stood out bright and sticky on the snow. And all too soon the boundary of our village wasn't enough. We moved out across Scotland as a pack of wild women, running untamed through the war-torn land. We took back the men and the boys that had been stolen from us: our fathers and brothers came home unharmed. We defeated all in our path with our superior strength and speed. No bayonet stab could wound us. No cannonball blast could make us flee. And no man could ever touch us unless we wanted him to. But I had always preferred women anyway. That's when I was happiest of all.

The start of something special

Jenny burst into the bathroom where I'd been lounging in the tub, relaxing after a hard day pushing papers in the office. "Have you heard what's happened to Mick and Sasha?"

"What happened to them?"

"Sasha found out Mick was into men." Jenny flashed me a wicked smile. "And when I say, Mick was into men, I mean he was really into men. Sasha came home to find him balls deep inside the postman. She's gone back to her mother."

"You're making that up," I murmured, sinking down into the sandalwood scented water. The thought of my friend, Mick screwing another man was just explosive.

Jenny hit me. "I'm not lying." She sat on the edge of the tub, rubbing her hands over my hairy belly. "Would you ever do something like that?" Her fingers wrapped around my cock. "I've seen the way you look at guys sometimes." I arched up into her silky hands before I could help myself. "I bet you want to bend some guy over your office desk, run your cock over his arse until he begs you to put it in him."

I felt my cheeks grow suddenly hot. "Where's all this come from?"

Jenny ignored my question, but her hands sped up as she squeezed and massaged me. "I'd be watching you both from outside, spying on you as you spread his legs. I'd spread my legs too, finger myself so I could come at the same time you did." Her eyes were big and wide. "That would be the hottest thing ever!"

I couldn't help myself. I erupted in the water, my hips bucking. There was no denying that I was turned on massively by my girlfriend's fantasy.

Jenny stood, and then she started peeling off her clothes. Her skin was flushed pink.

"What are you doing?"

"I'm going to get in the tub. I don't know about you, Roy, but I'm sweaty and feeling real dirty right now." She stepped into the water, sloshing it over the edge of the bath as she settled on my lap. I could feel my cock start to stir again.

I swept a lock of her long brown hair out of the way, and kissed the back of her neck. "I never knew you had fantasies like that. I never thought you'd want to see me with anyone else."

"Was I wrong? Because if I am, I won't take it any further." She held my hand, and then used it to stroke her breasts. She ground her bottom against my sensitive groin.

"You were right," I whispered. "I do think about men sometimes," I said nervously, still not believing that we were having this conversation. "I've never done anything though. I still love you."

Jenny nodded. "I want to see you with Eric, the milkman."

My cock suddenly woke up at the mere thought of that. Eric had been our milkman for years; he was more like a good friend than someone who delivered low-fat milk and pots of yoghurt to our house. Eric was also a tall strapping Scotsman with sparkling blue eyes, a constant smile on his face, and long legs that looked good even in his starched uniform.

"Eric would never go for it." I didn't know who I was trying to convince.

Jenny turned to kiss me. "Let me talk to him. This could be the start of something really special."

***

The Saturday after, Eric sat in our kitchen, drinking a cup of tea. Jenny nibbled on a slice of chocolate cake. I was too nervous to do anything. Our domestic scene looked the picture of normal, everyday life. That was until Jenny finished her cake.

"I bought some flavoured condoms yesterday. The banana one smells lovely."

Eric choked a little on his tea. "You're not planning on putting a piece of fruit up my arse are you? Because I'm not into that kinky stuff!"

I laughed at his joke, and then blushed. "We just want to practice safer sex, that's all."

"Well now," Eric said in a husky voice. "Why don't we go upstairs and you can show me how it's all done."

Jenny grabbed Eric with one hand, and me with the other. She dragged us bodily out of the kitchen, up the stairs and to the bedroom. I was gasping with excitement by the time I shut the door behind us.

Eric was no blushing virgin when it came to this. He pushed me up against the nearest wall, and then he kissed me, groping me all over as he did so with big strong hands. Kissing Eric was certainly different to kissing Jenny. The slight stubble on this cheek felt fantastic. I moved my hand down to his crotch, and pressed it over the bulge.

"Everyone get naked now," Jenny said, pulling her dress over her head. I'd never appreciated what a lovely little control freak she was, but I wasn't going to complain about it. I turned my back to everyone, feeling a little shy for some reason. When I undressed, and turned to face them, Eric and Jenny were already on the bed clutching at each other. My cock was impossibly hard from just watching the two of them. I wasn't going to last if just the sight of my girlfriend licking the milkman's balls was enough to undo me. When Eric pulled her up so he could pinch and twist Jenny's small nipples, I could hardly breathe.

Eric held out his hand, his eyes gazing at me. "Come here, lover." I ran over to the bed, and right into Eric's arms. The milkman French kissed me, pushing his tongue deep into my mouth. It felt so good that I wanted to climb on top of him.

I felt Jenny's hand stroking my cock, and then I looked down to see that she'd slipped a bright yellow condom on. "I've got strawberry and chocolate too." She winked at me. "I'm going to massage you now, sweetie," she said to Eric before she disappeared to his rear. "Make sure you're nice and slippery before my boyfriend gives it to you." I watched as Eric's eyes went glassy. He moaned with pleasure as Jenny moved her fingers like a pro, stretching and teasing his arse. I had to angle myself to take in the action, but it was a sight to be seen.

"Where did you learn all this stuff?" I asked Jenny, amazed at her skills.

"It's the twenty-first century darling. A modern woman has to know certain things." She twisted her fingers inside the milkman, thrusting deep and hard.

Eric was panting heavily, rocking into my embrace. "You're gonna make me come if you keep that up."

I held him by the balls, a firm but gentle pressure on the base of his cock. "You can come after I do. Is that a deal?" It wasn't actually that harsh of me. The way I was feeling now, I was ready to detonate like a bomb.

Jenny directed Eric to lay down with a pillow beneath his hips. She sat at the top of the bed, spreading her legs. I took in the sight of her furry mound, open and wet. Eric inched up to her, and then he started nuzzling and kissing his way to her crotch that was glistening and beautiful. I could have happily watched the two of them, but right then the sight of Eric's freckled arse was even more amazing. I kissed each of his arse cheeks, swirling my tongue over his skin. Eric smelt of tobacco and Paco Rabanne. I inhaled his scent with every sweep of my tongue. I couldn't wait any longer—I knelt between his legs, letting my cock find the way to his entrance. The head of my cock popped inside. I held myself still, enjoying the feel of it. A little pressure was all it took to make my whole body tingle. Eric arched up to meet me as I slowly sank inside his hot wet body. I could hear him make groaning noises but my girlfriend's thighs muffled the sound. Jenny's eyes were closed as Eric continued to lick and suck on her. But then she opened her beautiful brown eyes, and looked at me with pure bliss on her face. I sank all the way inside Eric, feeling like he was consuming me. I drew back a little, thrust inside again, but even as I did, I felt my brain start to short out like an electrical circuit with a power overload. I felt Eric clench around me as he came; the movements making me feel even more intense than I thought possible. I didn't last long but what I had was out of this world. I came hard, spurting out wave after wave of cum. My hips continued to buck when I thought I had nothing left. Eric took every last ounce of my strength; I literally collapsed on top of him. Jenny cried out shortly after, and then she sank back against the pillows. All three of us were sticky, exhausted but happy.

***

Eric was quiet as he dressed sometime later. I barely had the strength to move, so I sat in bed, feeling totally satisfied.

Jenny was curled up beside me, a happy look on her face. "Are you okay, Eric?" she asked.

Eric blushed bright red. "I didn't think it would be that much fun. I don't really want to go home now."

"Then stay with us for a bit," I said, waving him over.

"After all, I want to see you do my boyfriend," Jenny demanded in a voice that wasn't up for argument. Eric grinned, and then joined us on the bed, but I turned to Jenny in disbelief. She patted me on the crotch. "I want to enjoy every combination possible, if that's all right with you, darling?"

I was not going to be outdone by my girlfriend. "Eric," I said innocently, "Why don't we put Jenny in the middle next time?" I passed him a chocolate condom, holding it out of reach when Jenny tried to snatch it off me.

Eric put the condom in his back pocket. He unbuttoned his shirt, and then flung it on the floor. "As long as you do me again after, let's have some more fun!"

I put the last strawberry condom on the bedside table, and smiled to myself. My girlfriend had been right—this really was the start of something special.

Birthday wish

I told Lynnette that I wanted something special. It was my birthday, but I was always the giving kind. I wanted to give her something memorable. So after cake and karaoke, we went back to my flat where we had messy, noisy sex. I went down on her, lapping and sucking until she thrust against my face. But my lover's orgasm was just the start. I watched my girlfriend as she slumped back to the mattress in a sweaty heap. I needed her relaxed. She had to be chilled-out if I were to accomplish the things I planned. As she murmured happily in her post-orgasmic state, I guess I could have asked her for the keys to her beloved old car, and she would have just tossed it over right then. Lynnette was right where I needed her to be.

I wiped my sticky face on a corner of the bed sheet, and then I rummaged in my toy bag. I pulled on a pair of black latex gloves, and then I touched her once more. But when my fingers dipped inside, running in sweeps over her sweet pink vulva, I wasn't aiming for her well-sucked clit. I had something else in mind.

Lynnette looked down at me, flushed and breathless; she blew a long strand of her red hair from her deep blue eyes. "You've got to be kidding me." She looked at me with disbelief. "Baby, I'm done."

I squirted a generous amount of lube onto the palm of my hand, and then I raised an eyebrow. "I told you there was something special I wanted from you." I squished the clear goo until my girlfriend finally got the message.

Lynnette raised herself up on one elbow. "I thought you meant housework things, dog-walking things."

"I don't want you to walk my dog." Two fingers probed inside her, cutting her off from further complaint. "What I want is for you to enjoy this." I'd attempted to fist Lynnette on three separate occasions since we got together, but it had never worked out before. Nerves had been the main culprit on both sides, so this time I wanted it to be good for the two of us.

"Do you trust me?" I pushed my fingers inside a little more.

"Do you have to ask?"

"I love you," I said quietly. "I want to do this."

"Yes, Ma'am," Lynnette said, and the words were a gasp. Her chest expanded, her hips arched up, and then she slumped back on to the bed. "Just be gentle, okay?"

"Of course."

I smiled to myself. When I sucked her clit only a few minutes ago, my girlfriend was high and light; flying on a wave of pure pleasure. Now my technique had changed. I wanted to take her down, pull her inside her own soul. I wanted to make her growl. I closed my eyes, and all my other senses went south. My whole world circled wet and hot on the tips of my two fingers. When I added a third, slow and sticky, she humped my digits as if she were starving for sex. More lube, more pressure, and then I hit that sweet spot on the roof of her vagina; the spot that made her throw her head back with a almost silent scream.

My girlfriend had me trapped inside her, but why would I ever leave such a place? Some selfish part of me wanted to put my free hand between my legs, to rub and stroke my cunt at the sight and the feel of her, but I couldn't move beyond the in-twist-out motion of my fingers. Four fingers delved into the hot, wet space. Four fingers played my girlfriend like a one-woman orchestra. I took a deep breath when I realised that I'd been holding the air in my throat, silently entranced by the fisting experience.

"Look at me." My voice was a whisper. "Your cunt is beautiful. You are beautiful."

Lynnette clenched my fingers tight. I felt my own groin spasm in response. I was consumed. Her smell, her heat and all the small helpless noises she made drew me in further as I massaged her g-spot relentlessly.

On another day I'd try to insert my whole hand. On another occasion I'd fist her until she melted around me, but on that night, Lynnette purred and groaned, long and low as I brought her to orgasm again and again. Her climaxes were not sharp flashes of pleasure which she'd get when I concentrated on her clit. Rather when Lynnette came from fisting, her whole body shook, and I shook with her. We were joined hand to cunt; a single living entity that writhed on the damp bed sheets. And when she couldn't take any more, when she weakly hit me with a spare pillow, I simply placed my head on her thigh. My fingers slipped out after a while, but I stayed where I was, breathing in my lover. And every lungful of air had her scent within it, her fragrance that soaked into my skin and muscle and bone. This was what I wanted for my birthday; to feel like a new creation with the woman I loved.

Lynnette stroked her gentle hands over my plaited hair. "Of course you realise that I'm going to do you next," she said.

"You don't have to."

"It's your birthday." She squeaked a little as she sat up fully. "Just give me a moment, and I'll let you have your gift."

I crawled up the bed to kiss her on the lips. "Yeah, I'd like that." I kissed her once more. "I love you."

"You old smoothie," she said with a smile. "I love you too."

Life Drawing

"Rita, I need you to double-check this month's sales report." Harry, the store manager, held the door to his office open for me. I wasn't his secretary. I never went into his room to do any accounts. As soon as the door shut with a gentle click, he pulled me back to the battered metal filing cabinets. The rattle of draws was the only thing that gave away what we were doing. Harry squeezed my tits roughly, lifting one heavy globe out of my bra. He sucked on my dark brown nipple quickly, hands sliding down over the curve of my chest, then lower to my round belly. Harry never lingered there but only used the movement to push lower. I helped him out as I usually did; I hitched the hem of my skirt up, gave him access to the part of me that wanted this most of all. My pussy was hungry; when Harry shoved aside the fabric of my sensible knickers, I practically sucked him in. For all of his bad points, and I must admit there were a few; Harry was a genius with his hands. It wasn't too long before I bucked against the cabinet behind me, biting my lip to stop from crying out.

I let my natural instincts take over; I slid down to the hard floor where inertia, not desire made my head slump forward to his crotch. Usually a hand job would be quick and dirty enough for our office encounters, but that day my mouth opened automatically. Harry pushed inside, hissing as his cock slid against my tongue. He never lasted long when I blew him, but it made him happy. Keeping the boss happy offset most other factors, and in these times of economic troubles, I was all for that.

Of course there was a downside to my illicit fun. Harry barely acknowledged me outside his office. He said he wanted to protect my reputation. Right... I had a perfectly good full-length mirror at home. I'm fat, not stupid; Harry cared about himself and that was that. He shouldn't have worried anyway. No one thought we were having sex because no one thought that a big black woman like me ever had sex in the first place.

I sauntered into the staff room on Friday lunchtime. Kristine, the new girl was surrounded by the other workers. Everyone toasted her with fizzy wine.

"What's the occasion?"

"Kristine's just been promoted. She's assistant store manager now." Arnold passed me a plastic cup.

I ground my teeth together. Kristine and I were the only women who worked in the store, but unlike me, Kristine was white. She was also slender, with legs that were shapely, and tits that were perky. Kristine had a non-existent arse. She wasn't remotely my type, not that I was interested in women all that much.

"I've been here longer than most of the people in this room," I snarled. How come I didn't even get an interview?"

"Who knows what goes on in Harry's head," Arnold said quietly as our boss approached us.

"Harry, what gives? I'm a better sales person, I'm never late." I glared at him. "I never spend hours on the phone to my mates."

Harry looped his arm through mine, and led me away to a corner of the staff room. "Kristine has the right image that this store needs to project." He leered at her for a moment, and then turned back to me. "I mean, look at her. She's got designer labels coming out of her ear."

"This is Harry's Happy Computer Store, not Goldman and Sachs."

Harry fumed at me. "She's the stylish face that the public want to see."

I put my hands on my hips. "You're sleeping with her, aren't you?" A sudden image of Harry and Kristine in the throes of passion flashed up in my mind's eye.

Harry blushed crimson, but he plastered a tight smile on his face. "Don't be bitter, Rita. Don't make a fuss."

Someone passed round a plate of cupcakes; swirls of chocolate rose in peaks, all sweet and decadent. I refused one when Arnold offered it to me. I didn't have much of an appetite.

Harry nudged Arnold. "I'll have Rita's. She's probably on a diet anyway."

I clenched my fist, stared at Harry until he blushed once more and backed away.

"Don't listen to that idiot," Arnold said. "His time will come." He held his free arm out as if to hug me, but then his hand wavered. He smiled awkwardly, and then he stepped away.

No sooner had he gone that Kristine came over to me. "Rita, I hope we can still be friends."

I looked at her blankly. "This is the first time you've actually spoken to me. We were never friends in the first place."

"Well I never knew what to say to you. I didn't think we had much in common, what with our differences and all." Her eyes slipped down to my belly for a swift moment. "But now I'm your boss..."

"Harry's my boss."

Kristine hit me on the arm. "Harry needs to delegate more. But don't worry—we girls will always stick together." Her blue eyes went wide. "I know, let's go shopping after work. I know a lovely little boutique that sells wonderful Italian designs."

"I don't think so," I mumbled. Just the thought of spending any of my social time with her was annoying.

Kristine bit her lip. "You're right. I don't think they do anything in your size."

"Excuse me?"

Kristine screwed up her face. "Tell you what. My brother is married to a plump girl. I'll ask her where she gets her outfits from. We'll fix you up, just you see. There'll be no more tent dresses for you, dear."

I looked down at my outfit. Sure my black skirt was a little on the snug side, and my white blouse was nothing special, but everything was clean and pressed. I was presentable.

"Maybe some other time," I said, and then walked away. Stupid skinny cow!

I was useless for the rest of the day. I was aware of Arnold giving me strange looks but I was too wound up to pay him any mind. I wasn't even angry; I was just feeling sorry for myself. I knew that I was good enough to get another position elsewhere, so why didn't I do it? I just needed to pull myself together.

When six o'clock came, I strode out of the shop without a word. I walked slowly down the busy street surrounded by masses of shoppers. I realised I was looking at the ground when all I saw were pairs of feet; smart shoes, polished boots and the occasional pair of flip-flops. But then I spied a gorgeous pair of strappy heels. I raised my head, and was treated to the sight of luscious calves. I gazed higher to see a dark ruffled skirt that held wide sensuous hips. I almost walked into the object of my fascination at that point.

"Sorry," I mumbled like a fool.

The mystery woman steadied me. "No worries," she said with a smile. She had a wonderful Australian accent.

I suddenly felt about sixteen years old; this woman was gorgeous. My mouth opened and closed but my voice had dried up. I'd heard the phrase, *big and beautiful*, before but until then I'd never appreciated what it meant. I guessed that we were of a similar size; we were both curvy women, but she looked incredible with it. It also helped that she carried herself like a queen. I watched the beautiful woman walk further down Charing Cross Road, parting the heaving crowds before her with just the sway of her amazing hips.

My feet moved of their own accord. I tried to keep at a discreet distance, but I was totally smitten. Who was she? How did she manage to look so damn good, when compared to her, I looked positively dowdy? I'd honestly never seen a person of my size with such poise; such confidence and natural beauty. What was her secret?

The woman slipped into a doorway. I looked up at the building; it was Central Saint Martin's School of Art. I walked past and then doubled back.

A young man smiled at me as I entered the building. "Here for the open evening?"

"What?"

"The next tour starts in a minute. Which course are you interested in?"

"Um..." I looked around at the crazy sculptures that stood in the reception area. "I'd love to learn how to do something like those... things." I pointed at a monstrous-looking model made out of chicken wire and plaster.

"Then you're in for a treat." The young man ushered me to the back of a small group. "We have excellent facilities here."

I blindly followed the potential students as they oohed and ahhed their way around the ground floor. I didn't understand much of what was said as I was guided along, but I did recognise the names of a few painters the leader of the party mentioned: Gauguin and Rubens, names that made me smile as I dimly remembered the big women who featured in their paintings.

As we reached the back of the building I suddenly felt like an idiot. What was I doing wandering around with a bunch of teenagers? I broke away from the group as they reached yet another workshop full of crazy equipment and crazier teachers. I ducked into a darkened corridor, went up a flight of stairs but it didn't seem to lead anywhere. I looked around myself; I was well and truly lost. I tried to retrace my steps, and that's when I saw the words, *Life Drawing*, stuck to a door. Wasn't that where people drew naked models? I felt only slightly pervy when I cracked the door open to take a peek. My eyes grew wide as I took in the sight of the woman from the street who looked even more amazing for being completely nude, save for a silky red scarf that lay over one shoulder. I wasn't the only one mesmerised; all the students sat with happy grins on their faces as she walked to the raised platform in the centre of the studio.

The model sat on a big velvet chair, and then she arranged the scarf so that it sat draped over one breast.

I watched unseen as the students intently sketched the Australian goddess. The model reclined on a chair, one leg hooked over the solid arm. Her reddish hair fell down over her rounded shoulders like a copper cascade. My mouth dropped several inches as I took in her beauty just as I'd done earlier. But this time there were no clothes, save for the scarf in the way. This time I took in the sight of her juicy breasts with succulent pink nipples that contrasted with the blood-red of the fabric. I gazed at the curve of her tummy, the fleshy expanse that looked smooth and milky. My attraction to women had been with me since I was a teenager, but I'd never done anything about it. I never looked too closely at how I'd felt in the past, but right then I wanted to crawl over to the luscious queen, and lick every inch of her skin.

I slipped further inside the room. No one looked at me; all attention was focused on the model. I wished that I could swap places with her for just one moment; to hold court like her and be confident and sexy and so damn luscious. I screwed my eyes shut and made a wish. When I opened my eyes, the woman was looking right at me. I exhaled with the shock of it, but it came out louder than I thought.

A man approached me. "I'm sorry but this is a closed class."

I almost squeaked in response. I turned and ran. I was still breathlessly running when I encountered the tour party of potential students. I got directions back to the ground floor, and then I made a swift getaway.

****

I didn't get a wink of sleep that night. Every time I closed my eyes I saw the curvaceous queen beckoning me forward, her legs splayed wide so that I could see everything. I could practically smell her rich fragrance, and feel her smooth skin. I searched my memory, and remembered when I'd seen a book of prints by Gauguin when I was a teenager. The Tahitian women he'd painted had skin the same colour as mine, and they'd been big and beautiful too. These were the images that had decorated my mind when my appreciation of women had sparked as well. It was no accident that the two had happened at the same time. I pictured the large tropical women once more; they had confidence and dignity. They possessed so much beauty. I tended to keep the lights off when I got naked, but if I were ever bold enough to do what these women did, it would be bliss.

I jumped out of bed and switched on the bedside lamp. It was chilly in my bedroom, but I undressed anyway. I hunted in my wardrobe for anything silky. I found a thin patterned scarf, not as nice as the model's one, but it was enough for now. I dragged a chair in front of the mirror, and assumed a seductive pose. I looked stiff and awkward. I tried to relax. I changed position but it did me no good. I just looked like a fat lump with a polyester scarf on her shoulder.

I sighed out loud, got up and stood in front of the chair. I looked at myself in the mirror, turning this way and that. I ran my hands over my breasts; my nipples were hard in the chill of the room. I stroked over the pale brown squiggles of stretch marks that lay on my hips. I cupped my crotch without even thinking. I groaned when my forefinger slipped between the curly fuzz around my pussy to stroke over my clitoris. The scarf slipped from my shoulder but I managed to catch it as it dropped between my legs. I squeezed my thighs together, and then I pulled the cloth upwards. I shuddered as the scarf tickled my labia.

I had a wicked idea. I reached round, and tugged the scarf from behind. Gentle sawing motions made me tingle, whilst quick tugs made me quake. I wanted more. I tied several small knots in the fabric, and then I resumed masturbating; pulling the scarf from my clit to my arse. My eyes fluttered shut with pleasure, but when I opened them I saw someone new in the mirror—an image of the woman from the art class, or was it?

The life-drawing model had been white, whilst this voluptuous woman behind the glass had creamy brown skin and deep dark eyes. The reflection was neither Gauguin or Rubens, but a delicious combination of both.

I moved as if in a dream back to the chair. I placed one leg over the arm, and then I pressed the scarf inside my wet pussy as far as it would go. The thin cloth started to bunch up, so I massaged my whole crotch with it. I stared at the woman reflected, knowing that my wish to be someone new had been granted. I was a sex goddess; a queen who was strong and beautiful. I was worth more than a quickie in Harry's office. I was as priceless as a painting by Gauguin; a vivid piece of art with heavy sweeps of colour and rich decadent tones. I felt myself nearing my peak. I yanked the cloth from my pussy, dragging it over my fat swollen clit. I cried out as my whole body shook. I would never be the same again.

I staggered back to bed, holding the now-sticky scarf to my chest. I inhaled the smell of sex as I reached over to reset my alarm. The next morning I was going to get up early so I could check out the classified ads in the papers for a new job—something where all of my attributes would be appreciated. After that I'd do a little shopping. I'd treat myself to a silky scarf, and I'd wear it all day with pride.

Lead me to this place, but no further

The leafy avenues were full of fragrance. Flowers blossomed as a perfect vision, but as I stepped from my carriage I was full of dread. An assistant met me at the door, a young maid who smiled kindly. I tried to return one of my own, but I only quivered.

"Is your master in?"

"He's waiting upstairs, Miss Webster."

The maid took my trunk and other bags from my driver. I was somewhat surprised by her strength as she held everything in one hand. Long strands of her reddish hair fell in front of her eyes as she moved; she swept it aside with her free hand, and then she looked nervously at me. I left her to her duties, and ascended the stairs.

Doctor Stevenson greeted me warmly. "Now what's this?" he kissed me on both cheeks. "I won't have any tears." He seated me on a plush chair. "I promise your time here will be both restful and invigorating. When you leave, you will walk down the aisle as a happy woman."

I started crying at his kind words. I would never know happiness, I was sure of it. My impending marriage to General Clarence was six months away, but I was completely unprepared. The sea crossing from England to Rhodesia would take up even more of my precious time. I was certain that I would never survive.

I dabbed at my eyes. "My uncle said that you guaranteed positive results to my condition."

Doctor Stevenson nodded slowly. "My treatments are unique in the medical world. And for you, my dear, I will give my all. Your uncle is a man to whom I am in debt." He waved a hand about his head. "I won't bore you with stories from an old doctor. All I can say is that if it were not for your uncle, I would not be here right now." He shook his head. "We will discuss this further tomorrow. For now I want you rest. Lilly will show you to your room." The maid appeared at the door. "Call on her for everything you need. She is at your disposal, as am I."

I slept fitfully that night. My dreams were terrible; fears of my marriage and new life in Africa haunted me. I had never left England before. I knew nothing of the world. Who would I be able to turn to in that strange land? The marriage was an arrangement carried out with scant regard to my wishes. I shuddered as I thought of General Clarence, the stranger who would be my husband. Would he be a heartless brute like my late father? Or would he be an unfeeling soul like my uncle? These were the only men in my life. I could hardly imagine anyone different.

Eventually I did sleep. I awoke to find Lilly standing by the bed smiling down at me. She stepped back to reveal my washing supplies. I was still sleepy as I let her help me undress, but I gained sudden awareness when her hands swept over my breasts. Her actions were quite improper, but I could not help the way my body responded to her. My nipples became stiff and puckered. I gasped an urgent breath.

Lilly knelt at my feet, confusing me further. "The doctor says you're scared." She looked up at me, tilting her head to one side. "You mustn't be afraid of me though." Before I knew what was happening, her fingers pushed inside me with lightning speed. I almost collapsed as new sensations flooded me. I went up on tiptoes as she massaged me, and then she kissed me in the most private of places. I felt myself colour with shame and excitement as she pressed her face against me with urgency.

I pushed at her head, but she wouldn't move. "Enough," I said though my voice felt strained. "We must stop," I hissed, though it was my secret desire that the feelings never end.

"Do you really want me to stop, or are you being a stuck up cow?" Lilly grinned as she spoke.

"I beg your pardon?" This girl was intolerable.

"Your husband won't stop on your wedding night you know," she said. "You may as well enjoy yourself whilst you are able."

"Get out."

Lilly hung her head down but she left the room without further commotion. As soon as the door shut, I wedged a chair against it, and then sat on the bed. I looked down at myself; I never knew I was capable of feeling what I had just experienced. I dipped two fingers between my legs. I arched back on the bed. My hand moved of its own accord as I was consumed by pleasure. All the horrible things my father had told me about what lay down there rose up in my mind. He used to say all women possessed an 'evil honey trap.' God rest his soul, but he was a terrible liar. There was nothing but bliss that emanated from my sex. I would not deny myself this secret pleasure.

****

After breakfast the doctor led me to his consulting room.

"And how are we this morning?"

"I am much rested." I was surprised at how well I was feeling.

"Is Lilly giving you all you require?"

I flushed at that. "She is very dedicated."

"Now tell me, my dear, why are you here?"

""I want to be a good wife, but whenever I think of my intended, a terrible fear overwhelms me."

The doctor nodded. "This is quite common, but your journey into marriage is nothing to be afraid of. I am a medically trained physician as well a researcher into the human condition." He patted my hand. "I have prepared several bottles of an elixir for you to take if your nerves become extreme to the point of delirium." He picked up a small blue bottle. "I will provide you with a list of components for your chemist."

"Thank you, doctor."

"However there is more to your treatment than mere medicine," he said with a bright smile. "Now, my dear, please remove your undergarments and bend over."

"Excuse me?" Had I heard correctly?

"Your bloomers, my dear. You need to take them off if I am to examine you." He placed a hand to his mouth as if in realisation. "Of course, if you need Lilly to assist you, I shall call for her at once."

"No, please. I am quite capable." I stammered. "I just did not realise that an inspection would be necessary."

"There is more to being a wife than remaining calm, my dear."

I removed my underthings, and placed them neatly on a nearby table. The doctor turned his back as I disrobed. I bent over the chair, and coughed slightly to show that I was ready. I inwardly cursed my fears, and what they had led me to do. I felt completely exposed. I should not have worried though; the doctor was quite professional. That was until he pressed a finger to my posterior.

"Doctor!" I gasped. I felt the thick slide of grease against my opening, and then my eyes widened with shock as he pushed a cold metal object inside me.

"Now please rest assured; this treatment will have positive effects in the long term." He tapped the base of the object. "Relax the sphincter, and relax the mind. This is the modern approach to anxiety."

I could not respond as little explosions detonated behind my eyes. I convulsed as feelings, deep and powerful rolled through me. I tried to stand but I could scarcely manage. The doctor turned me about, and then pressed me down to the chair. I was instantly rewarded by a throb of delight. I was dimly aware when he spread my legs wide, but the feel of another smooth object against my sex brought me to full consciousness. This time when the wonderful sensations flooded me, I did not make it stop, or push him away. I fully enjoyed the feel of his instrument on me. I cried out as I experienced pleasure by his device alone.

"This is an invention of mine," he said proudly. "I call it, 'Quick Tempo Vibrational Stimulator.' The clerks at the patent office were most interested in its workings." The doctor sat back on his heels. "An orgasm is the most healing force in the world." He wiped his brow. "Even Florence Nightingale used to swear by them," he said with a laugh. I found that I could laugh with him. I felt so light and happy; something had loosened within me. My whole body was relaxed.

"Is this what all husbands do with their wives?" I asked. If my life was to hold this much pleasure then I would gratefully travel across the world to be wed.

However the doctor shook his head sadly. "Not all men are so considerate. In fact, your husband will not be kind."

"How can you know that?" I whispered

The doctor turned away. "Your uncle made me promise not to tell you. But I suspect that deep inside you must know the truth, and this is the real cause of your fears."

My heart seized at his words. I squeezed my eyes shut as I remembered overhearing the servants talk about the General; the horrified whispers of his cruelty that made me weak with dread.

"Your future husband has a terrible reputation. It is safe to say that you will need more than my elixirs when you marry. You will need a friend, my dear."

"A friend?"

"Lilly. She is perfect for you."

"That insolent girl is perfect for no one."

The doctor shook his head. "I promised your uncle that I would do all that was in my power to prepare you for your challenging life ahead. I even twisted the very laws of nature to ensure you would not have to go through it alone."

I looked up as I felt a shadow over me. Lilly looked down at me with a gentle smile. "He gave me some of his magic potions too."

The doctor stood, patting the maid on the shoulder. "Look at her. She is as strong as ten men." Lilly went over to the examination couch. She lifted the whole thing with just one hand. "Your husband will never strike you when Lilly is near. She is the finest example of science made flesh."

"This is impossible." Even after seeing Lilly's test of strength I still could not believe it.

"I told you not to be scared," Lilly said, kneeling at my feet. I could barely look at her, but then I felt her hand on my knee. I was still unclothed in front of this strange woman. I coloured with shame at my situation. "I'll look after you, Miss," she continued. "And I'll do all the things your husband never will." She kissed the inside of my thighs.

"Let Lilly finish what I have begun," the doctor said with an urgent tone.

I looked down at the maid, and placed a hand to her hair. She was very pretty. Maybe married life wouldn't be so horrid if I had a special friend with me.

"Is there no choice but to be wed?" I asked the doctor. "If you have such skill with your potions, could you not give me something that I may slip into my husband's wine?"

"Do you want me to poison him?" The doctor dabbed at his face. "I told your uncle that I would do anything, but I will not go to the gallows for you, my dear."

"No, of course not," I mumbled, suddenly ashamed for thinking such wicked thoughts.

"Your outlook is truly shameless," he spat. "You will be a respectable wife, and you will bear respectable children. Lilly here will stop any serious damage to your person. It is more than you obviously deserve, but your uncle has been most persuasive on the matter."

I felt overcome with emotion. No man could ever be trusted. But there was a woman at my feet, and she could well save me from future torment.

"Do you swear to protect me?" I asked her quietly. Lilly nodded. "And will you obey my every order?"

She smiled at me. "For as long as it pleases you, Miss."

I looked up at the doctor. "You said that orgasms have a therapeutic effect."

"That is true."

"Then I wish to have several more." I spread my legs wider. "Would you give me a moment to become better acquainted with my new friend?"

The doctor left the room with a strange look of relief on his face.

"Lilly if you'd be so kind?" The maid hoisted both of my legs over her shoulders. She bent her face to my sex, and then she proceeded to lick and suck at me much in the same way that she had done earlier in the morning. My new friend had some devious tricks that she played with her mouth; she nibbled at my flesh, bringing me to a state of bliss that was so strong, I could not see correctly when she was done.

"Thank you, Lilly," I said though my voice was weak from her exertions.

"It's my pleasure, Miss." Lilly crept up to kiss me. "I promise to look after you, so please understand that my next actions are in your best interest." Her lips lingered against mine, but after a bare second, she pulled me up quite roughly. "Put your knickers on," she said. "We're getting out of here."

"What?" I struggled into my bloomers, aware that I still held the metal device in my posterior.

"Doctor Stevenson is as crooked as the rest of them. If it wasn't for your uncle blackmailing him, he wouldn't be doing any of this. You'll only be safe with me, love."

I crossed my arms over my chest. "I will not be gallivanting anywhere with you. I have my responsibilities..."

"And what about your responsibility to yourself?" Lilly moved to the desk where she rooted about in a drawer. "You'll be the third wife the General had. They never found the bodies of the first two." She pulled out a large pile of money, and smiled brightly at me as she did so. "We've got cash, you've got class, and I've got muscle. Let them try to stop us." She stuffed the money into her bodice, and then held a hand out to me.

"Think you can make it out of the window?"

I stood open mouthed as the chemically enhanced woman showed me a possible future. I adjusted my skirts, and then I ran to the door. I wedged a chair against it with a single movement, sealing my fate. Lilly smiled, pulled open the windows, and then she led me out into a bright new world.

Debbie does BiCon

The room was heaving. The heat didn't make things any easier, but I squeezed inside the seminar room just as Winifred, the workshop leader pinned the 'session full' sign to the door. Sweat collected in my cleavage, making me wish I could just escape into a long cool shower. However there was no escaping this workshop; a last minute addition to a convention of bisexual activism, sci-fi, parties and perversity. It was my sixth time attending BiCon, however I hadn't learned a single thing in all that time. This year I had brought too many clothes, not enough money, and not a single drop of lube, although that wasn't such a problem as I hadn't had any offers for fun so far. If I couldn't get laid after this session, then I was handing back my bisexual identification card, and becoming a nun. BiCon was a great weekender, better than Christmas in some respects, but the current not-getting-laid part was frustrating too.

I really had no idea who would turn up to a session called, *Spanking for the fearful*; I was sure that most of the people crammed into the seminar room were seasoned veterans in the field of spanking. I'd come to this session straight after one called, *Bisexuality and Role-play*. There seemed to be quite a bit of a crossover between the lovers of fantasy and those who appreciated a well-tanned bottom. Some of the attendees had turned up to the session in costume: a green-skinned alien scribbled in a notebook, whilst someone in a silver robot outfit sat awkwardly on the edge of their seat. There were less outlandish attendees as well. I took in the sight of Thomas, or Master Thomas as he was sometimes known. The young man grinned like a crazy person as he took his seat. Thomas had been without a partner since his last submissive left to become a translator in Switzerland. I'd seen Thomas play before, and he was truly awesome to watch; he could handle a bullwhip like a professional. Thomas also had a sense of humility which was something sorely lacking in most dominant people I'd met. I wondered if he was looking for someone new to take under his wing, or if he was just after a good time like the rest of us.

The good time in question was in the shape of one Andrea Willis-Sobotka. Andrea was the most arrogant person I knew, period. She was also the most drop-dead gorgeous woman I'd ever come across, figuratively speaking of course. Andrea stood with her back to the rest of the room, head bent, hands crossed behind her back. She wore a black thong and nothing else. The temperature rose by several degrees as I appreciated the sight.

I loitered at the front for a moment, trying to get a better look, but Winifred distracted me with a wolfish grin. "I thought you'd be the first one here, Debbie, seeing that you have a crush on my beautiful friend."

"I'm too old for crushes, Winifred. I'm just here to observe." I wasn't fooling anyone, but I had to get my jollies somehow.

"You're a shit liar, Debbie. Don't ever play poker with me."

I nodded to where Andrea stood. "Is that how you got her to take part in your show-and-tell? Did she lose a bet?"

Winifred raised an eyebrow. "I just thought Andrea should donate a little of her time. Call it community service if you will for all the people she's pissed off. Now why don't you get comfortable and take a seat?"

I took the last chair available at the back of the packed room, waving to my friend, Hina, who wore a bubble-wrap dress—people kept reaching over to pop bits of her outfit, much to her visible annoyance. Hina was doing a Master's in Gender, Sexuality and Culture, so I was sure she'd get plenty of data for her research in this place. I was here for research purposes too, except my data would fuel my nightly fantasies. When I dreamt of Andrea spreading her legs so I could flick a crop over her thighs, I wanted to know exactly what shade of pink her skin would become. I wanted to mentally record the noises she made when she was being spanked so I could replay them in my head the next time I masturbated. My cunt wanted the full 3-D experience with quadraphonic sound. But since Andrea regularly ignored me as well as anyone not in her income bracket, I doubted that we'd be knocking boots anytime soon, so this would have to do.

Winifred placed a hand on my fantasy woman's shoulder, turning her to face her audience. Andrea's eyes grew wide as she took in the number of people present. The whole room suddenly grew hushed as everyone took in the sight of her round breasts, the curves and lines that led down over her stomach. The little dimple of a belly-button was perfectly placed, and below that was little more than a swatch of fabric that covered her cunt. The strip of cloth was the only thing that lay between her and a room full of eighty people. I could almost hear Andrea's shocked intake of breath as her situation hit home. But then she jutted out her chin defiantly, flicked her long dark hair, and struck a pose that would have lesser people scurrying for cover. Proud didn't start to cover Andrea Willis-Sobotka.

"I guess everyone knows what this session is all about," Winifred said with a low resonant voice. "Spanking for the fearful is an introduction to those of you who may be interested in impact play, and want to learn more." She grinned at the attendees. "But I guess most of you are here to see my beautiful friend be well and truly spanked!"

The crowd erupted into cheers. Andrea was blushing now; she looked straight ahead and refused to meet anyone's eyes. Winifred directed Andrea to a chair where she knelt on it with her side facing the eager crowd. There was a collective shift as eighty people leant forward at the same time. The temperature rose once more.

Winifred picked up an implement from a nearby table. She held it up for everyone to see that it was a short red strap.

"You can use lots of things to spank someone with," Winifred said almost conversationally. She swung the strap with a graceful back-hand. Andrea remained motionless as the length of leather impacted on her backside. "This strap is easy to control. It's a nice beginner's tool." She struck down twice more, one on each of Andrea's arse cheeks. "I could do this all day and not get a sore arm." Winifred brought the strap down with more force. The person sitting next to me flinched at the noise. I only grinned as a red outline appeared over Andrea's bottom. "Of course you could always start off with your hand," Winifred stated. "Go with whatever is the most effective." She placed the strap in her back pocket, and then struck Andrea's bottom with her hand. For a split second I could see the shape of her fingers and palm print on the pale woman's skin, but then I blinked and it was gone. "How are you doing, darling?" she asked.

"Fine," Andrea growled.

Winifred stepped back and smirked at the kneeling woman. "Spankings aren't just for punishments—they can be used to give pleasure too. I'm having a great time, Andrea as we've all heard is doing just fine and dandy…" she paused and looked right at me. "But as this is a very hands-on session, I'm sure one of you would like to help me out."

My hand shot up in an instant. I hopped up and down until Winifred smiled and nodded at me. "Debbie, please do us the honour."

I practically leapt out of my seat, and scrambled down to the front of the room. Master Thomas gave me the thumbs-up as I made my way past him.

Andrea gave me a sideways look, and then looked away. "She's not so scary," she muttered.

"Oh, I think you're going to enjoy yourself, Debbie," Winifred crooned. She waved her hands at the implements displayed on the table. "Knock yourself out, sweetie."

"I think I'll use my bare hands." The words had scarcely left my mouth when I landed a loud slap to her thighs.

"That's nice," Winifred commented. "Can everyone see? You don't have to just spank the bottom. Thighs both front and back make a lovely target."

I continued to spank Andrea with all the energy I had. There was no warm up, no steady increase; just full-strength blows that made the arrogant beauty shudder. After about a minute Andrea began to moan quietly.

"Are you okay?" I asked, although I was feeling quite satisfied with myself.

"Just peachy," she snapped.

I grabbed a handful of her hair, and angled her head back. "What did you say?" Andrea screwed up her face with disapproval, but said nothing. "I think I'll make you count the next ten I give you." I'd fantasised about doing this ever since I'd first seen Andrea at last year's event, but this was so much better than my daydreams or my afternoon and evening dreams either.

My cunt tingled with delight as I thought of all the power I had right there and then. "You can count, can't you?" I winked at the assembled crowd who laughed out loud.

I brought down my hand on her arse, revelling in the sting against my palm followed by the warmth that blossomed beneath my hand.

"One," Andrea said with gritted teeth.

I turned to Winifred who held her sides as she chuckled. She handed me a flat paddle, a little like a ping-pong bat. "Save your hands and use this instead."

I tapped the paddle against my thighs, weighing it up as I walked around Andrea.

"Spread your legs wider," I said, nudging her legs apart.

"I'll fall off the wretched chair if I do," she complained, shooting me a dirty look.

"Fine. I'll just have you over my knees then." I directed her to stand, and then I sat down on the chair. "Come on, princess." I patted my thighs.

Andrea rubbed her bottom for a moment before she placed herself over my lap. I wished that I could slip my fingers inside her cunt, but this was spanking for the fearful, not fisting for the fearless. This may be the closest I'd ever get to Andrea, but I was still aware that there was a room full of people, aliens and robots all watching me. But then I realised that they weren't watching me at all. All eyes were glued on Andrea; all eyes except for Master Thomas who smiled an encouraging smile at me. It wasn't enough though. I felt suddenly empty; as if none of this was real. Was I nothing but an extra in this scene? I exhaled a long breath, feeling bone- tired.

Andrea craned her head to look at me. "Well hurry up with it," she hissed. "I don't want to miss the next session."

I spanked her nine more times, hardly listening when she counted out the strokes. My heart wasn't in it. When the conventioneers clapped I felt like they were being polite. My fantasy woman was a complete cow although some of it was my fault; I should have stayed at the back of the seminar room and fantasised about Andrea instead of getting up close and personal.

Winifred seemed to pick up on my change in mood. She squeezed my shoulder. "Thanks, Debbie, you did great." She helped Andrea to stand, before she turned to the rest of the room, "No why don't we all split into two groups: those who want to receive a spanking on one side, those who want to give one on the other."

There was a mad rush of movement as everyone hurried over to opposite sides of the room. I stayed where I was, seated on my chair at the front feeling totally lost.

"Spankers and spankees, go find each other. I'll mingle and answer any questions." Winifred led Andrea away to the side where she wrapped the spanked woman in a long red kimono. Neither of them looked at me.

I stood. My legs moved of their own accord as I walked amongst the crowd. I watched as the silver robot spanked an older black man. The green alien had finally put down their notepad, and was now bent over a table whilst two others conventioneers slapped each of its arse cheeks in unison. Everywhere I turned people were fearlessly enjoying the pursuit of spanking. But what about me? I'd been stupid to be so obsessed with Andrea; that stuck-up cow wouldn't ever look at me the way I looked at her. She didn't want me.

Master Thomas appeared in front of me. He still had a huge grin on his face. "That was just the hottest thing I've ever seen," he said, and then he just stood there, looking at me with a strange expression on his face. "I was wondering if you'd like to you know..."

"You know what?" I blinked. "I don't think that would work out. I'm more of a giver of spanks, not a receiver. I can't imagine you bending over and taking it from anyone."

"You're not just anyone as you so ably demonstrated." He smiled and looked down at his feet. "And I'm not such a dyed-in-the-wool dominant that I can't bend over as it were, when the right opportunity presents itself."

It took me a moment to decipher his mumbling words. He looked up at me shyly, and when he did, his dark brown eyes were focused completely on me. I felt the open desire in his voice; my clit pulsed with renewed strength. The longing for Andrea Willis-Sobotka didn't instantly disappear from my mind, but as I held out my hand, her influence reduced considerably. "Come with me." Thomas gripped my fingers, and exhaled with relief.

"Oh thank god. I thought you were going to tell me to get lost."

"Nah, but I would like to take you back to my room so I can really see you bend over."

"For a spanking?"

"Of course," I said innocently. "What else where you thinking of, and does it involve lube?"

Thomas leaned in close to whisper, "When I picture you flogging me and then pumping your fingers into my arse, there's always lots of lube involved. It's a good thing I brought an enormous bottle with me."

"Naughty boy. I think I may enjoy this." I rubbed my sore hands together with glee.

Thomas grinned. "Ah, Debbie, I've been thinking of a lot of things that we could do together. I've been thinking of you for quite some time."

"Yeah?" I was absolutely shocked, but then I recovered myself. "Of course you were thinking of me. I'm great, if I say so myself."

Thomas and I ran from the room and straight back to mine. BiCon was better than Christmas after all. It was about time I celebrated that.

Property is theft

Before the sun had yet risen, the three of us descended from the wall. The supermarket was quiet, eerie with shadows. Around the back, vast quantities of discarded food lay at our feet, stored in skips before being disposed of the next day. We moved as one unit; too small to be a flock, but unified with a single thought: get the food home before the sun comes up. What we did wasn't stealing, but it wasn't exactly a spree either. The bird-people, the skippers, the dumpster-divers—people called us by all sorts of names. I liked to think of us as urban harvesters. With the help of our handy-dandy crowbar, nothing could stand in our way. A feast was within our sights.

Joe and Ansel scanned the area as they moved, each one headed in their chosen direction. Joe spied loaves of bread just past their sell-by date, bags of avocadoes, dairy-free doughnuts, and enough fruit to feed a small but hungry army for days. Food in all of its colourful glory disappeared into backpacks, and all the while, we worked with an ear tuned to unfamiliar footsteps; to the one-eyed light of a security guard's torch.

Our movements slowed as our bags gained weight, but we were as quick as we could be; an efficient threesome.

If people are treated as property, and all property was theft, then where did that leave a transient gal like me? I'd been drifting for so long that it hurt sometimes, but the fear of being tethered scared me more.

"I had a dream last night," I said, hefting several oranges into my bag; the citrus smell was sweet and fresh. "I was the winner of a supermarket dash, but it was in a shop that sold only chocolate cake. Then as a reward I got a key to the vault."

Joe straightened his back. "We used to make chocolate apples back home. My family's orchard was always trying to find new ways to use up the surplus crop."

"I've never had a chocolate apple before," I said as I flexed my bad knee. "And I just can't imagine you on a farm."

"It was an orchard, not a farm," Joe snapped. "I'm sorry," he whispered, looking down.

"That's okay." I only knew a little about what Joe had escaped from, what he'd left behind when he ran from the orchard and into our arms. I knew he liked to sleep with his back to the wall; that he had a little boy barely hidden beneath layers of angst.

"There were trees that just went on forever. I used to think the whole world was like that—fruit and cider and hot farm boys." He sighed, looking somewhere I could not see. "Stupid, but I miss it so much sometimes."

Ansel strode over to us, silently placed a hand on Joe's back. Ansel's dreadlocks swished this way and that as he moved to kiss us both on the forehead. He didn't speak much at all, but we knew he was ours and we were his. And if people were property, and property was theft, then we would all end up in jail.

Later Ansel cooked soft polenta as Joe and I slept in the bed. I awoke to the smell of warm and tasty food. Love and affection was heavy in the air. I felt anchored to the men in a way that made me suddenly scared. But then my fear was swept away when Ansel crept silently into the bedroom with bowls of breakfast. I spied yellow mush topped off with avocadoes and tomatoes, sweet and ripe. I tasted the sun, salty, smoky and bright with every mouthful I ate. Joe sat on Ansel's lap, and then the two men fed each other spoons of the meal until their mouths were sticky and their dicks were hard. I knelt at their feet, though the floor was cold. I stroked hands up, down, and then up once more to capture the bulge that pressed against Joe's shorts. A kiss came next as I nuzzled deeper, swept my tongue over his freckled skin. We cooed like bird-people; moved as one unit with a single goal: make Joe come hard. I slurped along his thighs whilst Ansel flicked a tongue across his nipple. The kisses continued until Joe gripped Ansel with one hand, me with the other, holding my head steady as I swallowed gulp after gulp. Nourishment moved between us. Love flowed free and sweet. I slumped against my lover's legs, but my eyes still drifted to the window; to whatever lay in the world outside.

****

If people are property and property was theft, then two men owned my heart completely. I may not like the idea of being chained around my heart, but this was something I could not escape, even when I wished that I felt nothing. We went out several nights later. Things should have been normal, routine, but bad things happen to good people all the time. Ansel is a six-foot five ex-Rasta, with skin the colour of burnt sugar. He stands out wherever he goes. Nobody ever thinks he could be as gentle and loving as he is. A big black man had to be a crook, right? I only knew something was wrong when I heard heavy footsteps. I hid behind a dumpster, and saw to my shock, a security guard carrying Ansel's bulging back pack. Joe, who was crouched beside me made a move forward, but I stopped him with a whisper. "It won't do us any good if we all get arrested." I saw the crowbar in his hands, saw the way his knuckles curled in a tight grip. I knew what he was thinking, but violence had never been our way. He sagged against me, defeated.

Two uniformed men pushed our silent lover into the back of the supermarket. I saw Ansel briefly glance in our direction as he passed by our position; a sliver of hope that we would not be found. When the door slammed shut, I felt a shiver all over my body. We sat there huddled together for hours, but then we were forced to leave as the day grew brighter. We made our way home. Our rooms felt bare, sterile. Joe and I climbed into bed, but neither of us wanted to move to the space where Ansel usually slept. We gripped at each other, fingers pressing so hard that little pink smudges blossomed on our skin. We tangled the sheets; kissed with ferocity—just enough pressure to stop my fearful thoughts from coming to life. Panicking wouldn't help me.

"Ansel." I had to say his name as my orgasm thundered through me. Joe's knee was wedged to my groin, glued to my clit. My fingers wrapped around his cock. I squeezed my eyes shut, praying that our lover would be safe. Our primal offering of sex became a sacrifice. It was all we had to bring our man home. I hoped whatever deity looked down on us would accept it, for we had nothing left to offer. Everything I owned lay in the four walls of the room. But part of my heart was somewhere else I could not see. My world felt fractured and small.

Joe pumped warm and sticky over my skin, shaking as he whispered Ansel's name. We rolled apart from each other, the sheets suddenly cold. The bed felt far too big. I slept, but nightmares thrashed about my head. I pictured Ansel, beaten on the floor; his dark locks stained with red. But when I blinked my eyes open, with lashes wet from tears, I saw Ansel sitting at the bottom of the bed smiling at me.

For a moment, I thought that I was still dreaming, but then I scurried to his arms, squeezed and kissed him. I knew that he was real. Our movements woke Joe. Soon long arms went around us both. We held each other as a single entity, relieved and so very happy.

"What happened?" I asked. "What did they do to you?"

Ansel laughed deep and low, swept my hair from my eyes. "They made me cook breakfast."

I opened my mouth, but nothing came out. Ansel disentangled himself from us, although Joe took some convincing to let go. The darker man undressed, and got into bed; his rightful place was in the middle. We weren't about to let him go again.

"We had a deal," Ansel continued. "I cook them the best breakfast they've ever eaten, and they don't prosecute my ass."

"What did you cook?" I snuggled close.

"Crisp cornmeal waffles, sweet balsamic tomatoes, hot and spicy mushrooms, and red flannel hash. It was pure Ital."

Joe kissed him hard. "You crazy, brilliant man."

"Damn right." Ansel was hands down, the best cook I knew. And now he was back where he belonged; back with us. We ran hands over his chest and through his hair, touching and stroking to ensure he was real. Affection moved between us. Love flowed free and sweet.

I sat astride Ansel's hips. He felt solid beneath me; not a bird-person at all, but human and real. I sank on to him slowly. Ansel was a big man. My cunt stretched to hold his cock as I moved up and down. Joe lay beside Ansel, kissing his chest, swirling his tongue over dark brown nipples. Ansel bucked up, planting himself deep inside me. I rocked to and fro, massaging my g-spot with every rough jerk of my hips. Ansel became silent as he thrust up harder and harder. Little beads of salt-sweat appeared on his face, his biceps grew taut and stiff. I smelt his fragrance—cooking scents and musk; heady and intoxicating.

I felt myself come for the second time that day. My orgasm radiated out from my belly, filling up all the empty places until I literally hummed from its power. The chains of love I'd feared shifted, morphed until they became wings. I flexed and shook as freedom lifted me, made my heart swell and sing. My men looked up at me with broad smiles. Joe reached up to squeeze one breast, whilst Ansel stroked the other. I felt a second wave begin; the connection with my lovers was too intense for me to ever want to escape. Power travelled from fingers to nipples, from cock to cunt. We moved and gyrated as a single unit with one goal in mind: make me soar; make me fly.

"Don't ever scare us like that again," I said breathlessly as I rolled off Ansel. He kissed my hand, covered me with the blanket. I was suddenly hungry for toast and jam, but food could wait. This was where I belonged, with my head resting on Ansel's chest, and my hand clasping Joe's wrist beneath the covers. We were not each other's property. We were all simply in love. And the last time I checked, love was totally free.

More titles by Jacqueline Applebee

Sweet Pet (Shadowfire Press)

http://tinyurl.com/5mqrym

Geon is desperate to be free. Can Stephan's love release the shapeshifter from his cage?

Geon is a Shapeshifter, raised by humans, but kept like a pet. His new owner, Robert wants to use him for his own pleasure, and to entertain friends, but Geon dreams of a life beyond being Robert's personal sex toy.

As Christmas draws near, Geon escapes into the arms of a stranger named Stephan. Together they enjoy intense passionate encounters that leave both men hungry for more. However, Robert wants his pet back, and he thinks nothing of using force and blackmail to snatch the shifter away.

Stephan takes matters into his own hands when he sets out to rescue his new lover from the clutches of the powerful man. He uses an innovative and sexually charged plan to make sure that when the New Year rolls around, Geon will be free forever.

Sweet Pet 2: Battle Cry (Shadowfire Press)

http://tinyurl.com/y9hslyv

Will a new shapeshifter make Geon's dreams come true, or give him nightmares?

There's a new shifter in town. Geon becomes obsessed with meeting this new creature, and will do anything to find him. However, Geon's lovers, Stephan and Danny would prefer him to stay out of sight with them.

Stephan and Danny are torn between protecting their lover, and letting him learn about others of his kind. The men have to trust their sweet pet that he will do the right thing, even if their instincts make them want to drag Geon back to bed for some more hot sex.

On Christmas Eve, Geon learns of his true origins, but to see more he must leave his lovers just as their three-way relationship reaches an intense stage. The new shifter is sexy, strong and smart. He seems to have all the answers Geon needs, but is he too good to be true? Geon has to risk everything to discover the facts for himself.

Angel on the roof (Shadowfire Press)

http://tinyurl.com/mc5lj5

As an earth elemental, Penny's orgasms make the whole world move!

Penny's hidden herself away for too long. When psychics start falling victim to a heartless attacker, it is up to her to stand up to an evil foe. With the help of a sexy juggler, she embraces her elemental power, and lets a fallen angel fly once more.

Erotic Brits (eXcessica)

http://tinyurl.com/4xxkayb

If you ever thought the United Kingdom was a nation of stiff upper lips, then prepare to learn what really gets hard in the U.K. This unique collection celebrates all the naughty exploits that take place up and down the county, including women who love to have kinky fun in a queer London pub, and a threesome who enjoy outdoor sex at historic Edinburgh Castle. The locations don't only provide a backdrop to the lusty scenes-they become an integral part of every sizzling story. This tour is not in the guidebooks, but you can take it right now!

Ripper's Redemption

http://tinyurl.com/4xd3zfp

Is Jack the Ripper alive today? Jessie is happy leading a hedonist lifestyle, with plenty of women to enjoy in or out of her bed. When Jessie's friend asks for help in finding her missing lover, Jessie is reluctant, however as increasing numbers of women go missing in the East End of London, she is forced into action. Jessie barely starts her investigation when she realises that she is being watched by a mysterious figure. With the help of her friends, and a ghostly visitation from her Aunty, Jessie learns that there is a connection with these recent disappearances, and the unsolved mystery of Jack the Ripper.

Erotic Brits 2: Sexy Scotland

http://tinyurl.com/3zoz22b

Fancy a Highland fling? This anthology showcases a sexy Scotland for your pleasure.

• Glasgow by the back door: Kinky fun awaits a newlywed on her honeymoon, when she learns that it's always the shy folks who love anal.

• Up Helly Aa celebrates the Viking history of the Shetland Isles in a fiery tangle of sex.

• Celtic Tongues: A woman joins a threesome at Loch Ness with two Gaelic-speaking lovers.

• The Blackening sees a friendship renewed, and then some when a visitor takes part in the ancient Pagan ritual of blackening a bride-to-be before her big day. There are plenty of opportunities to get naked and dirty in this tale.

• Scottish grub: The unique cuisine of Scotland is explored one sexual encounter at a time. However sex and food is a partnership made in heaven, so good taste wins in the end.

• Local Colour: A hidden heritage is discovered where a woman learns to love submitting to her Master.

• The Middle sees a threesome play out their sexual fantasies on the beautiful Isle of Skye.

• Scotland the brave: a fan of the film, Braveheart works as a gigolo. He meets his match in a woman who loves William Wallace just as much as he.

Fallen Soldiers

http://tinyurl.com/3cgxtvj

Love can bring you home, no matter where you are. For Sarah, love spans the barrier of death, to bring two fallen soldiers back to the present.

Ernest and Albert are ghosts, each freed from statues that held their essence by Sarah, who possesses an amazing ability, unknown to anyone including her.

Sarah's boyfriend Leo has rejected her, and now all she wants to do is to lose herself deep in the English countryside, but instead of solitude, she finds an erotic adventure, and so much more. When one of her friends mysteriously disappears, Sarah has to learn how to fight for the people she cares about, and finds an inner power that makes her strong enough for any challenge. She is rewarded for her bravery by the love and support of her lovers, both living and undead.

The Concealed Man

http://tinyurl.com/3ts6lnw

What would you conceal from the one you loved? What would you reveal?

Patrick and Lee discover love in the unlikeliest of places, when they meet after a friend's funeral. Patrick only has anonymous sex with faceless men, whilst Lee has learnt that pleasing others is the only way to survive. Despite having a supernatural ability to move into solid rock, Lee's life has been full of violence and neglect. Lee secretly lives in a cemetery, keeping a watchful eye on the mourners who feel that they cannot go on without their loved ones.

Both Patrick and Lee have hidden a part of themselves from the world, but together, they discover a passion that neither had ever thought possible. Their love leads them from the heart London to the edge of Britain. On their journey they are able to uncover the secrets of Lee's ability, and his concealed family who live in the shadows of the rugged Atlantic coast.

Illuminate Me

http://tinyurl.com/3gv2jta

Illuminate Me. Tell me about sexy men who knit; the rare souls who love yarn with a passion. Enlighten me. I want to hear about a woman who uses silence to convey her desire. Tell me about the bound, struggling girl in a cocoon of soft cloth, and the friends who teach each other how to suck cock. Teach me how time and space spirals from a marker on the ground. I want to know about the wet kiss, bitten lips, groping, moaning, screw till you're sore tales you've written.

Contains six of my favourite stories that have appeared in previous anthologies

- **Knit one, purl two** Bondage and Knitting are not so strange bedfellows...
- **Old London town** A woman finds she's a useless tour guide, but there are other ways to keep her visitor happy in the big city.
- **Logic** Just how is a woman supposed to learn how to give head? By learning from her best friend, of course...
- **Tight Sweater** A figure-hugging sweater that won't come off? Don't worry, love, the woman upstairs will be happy to rip your clothes off!
- **The Flicks**Lots of naughty fun can be found at the local cinema, especially when the lights go down...
- **Hush** Silence is an aphrodisiac. Silence is power. Ball gags and a horny professor are just plain fun!

Teardrops

http://tinyurl.com/443lfjc

Are you only happy when it rains? Sad tales of desire occur to me more than I wanted people to know; much more than seemed fitting for a happy-go-lucky creator of erotic fiction. Be aware, there are more than kisses and flowers when it comes to lust. There are pierced hearts, wilting roses, and the ever present drip-drops of tears.

Contains the following brand new stories:

- Dancing in the dark: you hit rock bottom, but redemption is waiting in the arms of two men who love you...
- My mother's voice: the echoes of violence carry on through the years, but hope for a brighter future comes from the most unexpected of places.
- Pieces of me: a disabled woman lives in a paranormal world where nothing gets in her way when it comes to sex!.
- Boys next door: your average Welsh boy finally gets to live out his fantasy with the boys next door, but will it make or break him?
- British Summertime: a flood is approaching, but more importantly, can you have sex with both of your lovers before the waters hit?
- Muscle Memory: the fear of growing old enables one woman to experience a variety of sexual experiences that she will never forget.

An Expanded Love

http://tinyurl.com/3eo5pep

How big is your heart?

Nadia asks herself the same question. When she meets Christine, she learns that monogamy isn't the only way to have a relationship. Christine is polyamorous; she dates more than one lover at the same time, with the knowledge and consent of everyone involved. Nadia decides to try this way of relating for herself, but her first steps into polyamory are terrifying, exhilarating and strange. The jealousy she feels over sharing Christine with another woman goes out the window when Nadia falls for a Pagan synchronised swimmer, Yolanda, and her cookery-obsessed boyfriend, Sam.

More relationships can mean more love, but it can also mean more drama. When Yolanda's crossdressing child, and Nadia's moody ex-boyfriend get thrown into the mix, things get rather interesting...

Polyamory may be a new word, but loving more than one person at the same time is nothing new. This is not your standard romance.